HOURS with the MAST

BOOK 5 • GRADE 6

GW00373006

BOSWORTH EDITION
part of The Music Sales Group

Allemande

(from Suite No.16 in G minor)

This must be vigorous and buoyant, with a bright accent on the first and third beats of each bar. Make a clear distinction between the staccato notes and the smoothly flowing semiquavers of the motive figure, wherever it appears, but carry forward the musical thought as shown by the long slur over the first few groups.

HANDEL
1685-1759

Made in England
Imprimé en Angleterre

Tous droits d'exécution réservés
B.& Co.Ltd.19613

Allegro
First Movement from Sonata in A

Light, rhythmical treatment is needed for this, with rather percussive touch to give brightness of tone.   Most important features are forward progression of all short notes to the accent, crisp staccato in contrast to legato and tone grading as marked.

ARNE
1710-1778

Sarabande

From French Suite No.1 in D minor

The best way to study this is to play each line of notes as a separate melody, and listen carefully to every detail of time, tone and touch. Then, when playing it as written, see that every part has its true character as though played by a string quartet. Good *cantabile* tone is needed; *tempo* broad, but flowing enough to give an easy grace to the sequential figures. Attend to small details within the long phrase marks. Interpret *mesto* as rich and fully sustained rather than *heavy*.

BACH
1685-1750

Allemande & Air

From French Suite No.4. in E flat

Notice that the phrases, and many of the semiquaver groups, begin on a weak part of the beat, and take care that these notes are softly played and that they lead directly to the more important note.   See that R.H. is held well over the keys, so that black and white keys may be played with equal fluency.   Pay great attention to part-playing, and see that long notes have more initial tone than short ones, so that they will sing for their full time value.   L.H. low notes must sing out well.   The *Air* must be light and very rhythmical.

BACH

Air

From French Suite No.4. in E flat

BACH

Prelude in E minor

The melody must be played with very *cantabile* tone; the L.H. chords smooth and *close* to give an effect of orchestral colour, with surgings and ebbings of tone within a fairly small range of contrast. The pedal must be changed whenever the harmony or the *melody* changes, exactly as marked. The small notes in bar 16 are played rapidly before the beat, leading into a strongly singing G natural.

CHOPIN, Op.28, No.4.
1810-1849

Largo espressivo ♩ = 84

Solfeggietto

First study the harmonic structure upon which the single notes are built.   This will enable you (a) to shape the hands rightly over their keys and accomplish the *joints* between various groups neatly; (b) when playing the semiquavers rapidly to make the harmonious background clear to the listener.   See that all runs go straight into the next bar.   Fluent finger touch and light hand needed.

C. P. E. BACH
1714-1783

Albumleaf in E flat

From "Bunte Blatter"

As this is to be played with a certain amount of *rubato* the metronome speed must be taken as approximate only. The *rubato* must not distort the rhythm, but must be taken as a gentle swaying of the time line. The first two phrases after the double bar may be played with a slightly more animated effect. Small notes to be played rapidly before the beat. Part-playing needs the greatest care, so that the tone of each individual voice is carefully matched, and every note held for its full value.

SCHUMANN, Op.99.
1810-1856

Le Coucou
Rondo in E minor

A bright rhythmical forward movement is of the utmost importance here. The *cuckoo* notes to be clearly articulated wherever they appear, with special attention to the upper R.H. notes in such places as bars 2, 3, etc., where the *cuckoo* is hidden. Tone gradations must be constant, but on a small scale - delicate, never heavy.

CLAUDE DAQUIN
1694-1772

B.& Co.Ltd. 19613

La Commère

Here are two busybodies gossiping and chattering one against the other.   This gives the clue to the rendering.   Long slurs show the phrasing.   Attend to all details within these slurs.   Very rhythmical.

COUPERIN
1668-1733

May, Charming May!

If every detail of touch contrast, phrasing and tone colour is observed a lovely deli-
cately-lined picture will result.   See that the *half-staccato* notes are only *just* detached,
and that they speak clearly.

SCHUMANN, Op.68. No.13.

Fantasia in C

Brightly rhythmical throughout.　　Bring out the melodic figure formed by the lower
R.H. notes of semiquaver passages, bars 5, 7, 9, 10 etc., keep the upper notes quiet.
Attend to the syncopations in bars 21-24, but look after the normal accent in L.H.

HANDEL

Andante

From Sonata in G

Announce the theme very simply; guard against hurrying.   Be careful to bring out
the theme wherever it appears in the variations, especially when it is in the inner voices
and L.H. part.   Let the *sf* notes be really strong, with tone tapered on the next sound.
Final chord full and strong.

BEETHOVEN Op.14. No.2.
1770-1827

Andante ♩ = 84
La prima parte senza replica

12.

Fantasie - Dance

The first note of each set of triplets must be strongly accented, the others played lightly, so that those first notes give an effect of melodic outline. Carefully observe tone gradations in the L.H. *cantabile* melody of second section, and colour the R.H. accompaniment brightly. Joyous forward rhythmic impulse throughout.

SCHUMANN, Op. 124.

Catch Me If You Can
from "Scenes of Childhood"

The R.H. part requires very good finger independence, with firm tips to transmit energy, backed by hand touch for the accents.   The *sf* followed by *p* should be carefully observed, and all staccato notes unmarked should be light and *fugitive*.   The single bass notes should have special attention.

SCHUMANN, Op.15. No.3.

14.

B.& Co.Ltd.19613

Three-Part Invention

This should be played expressively, with clear singing tone in all the parts. Care is needed accurately to time the sustaining notes and the entry of short notes following a rest, also
in the matching of tone when the melodic line of any part is shared by the hands.

BACH

B. & Co. Ltd. 19613

Waltz in B minor

Both notes in all of the groups of thirds must be equally clear; accents should be bright, and tone-contrasts between the stronger and lighter bars carefully observed. Grace notes are played rapidly on the beat, throwing a strong accent upon the principal sound.

BRAHMS, Op.39. No.11.
1833-1897

Allegro moderato ♩ = 126

B. & Co. Ltd. 19613

Song Without Words

Where the semiquaver melody corresponds with the third note of the triplet in the accompaniment it is Mendelssohn's own indication, and it would be quite in order to make all similar figures coincide, even when not so marked. The melody must flow easily and very smoothly, and the accompaniment, though subordinate, must have tonal variety, with warm, full tone on the low bass notes - the real bass.

MENDELSSOHN, Op.85. No.1.
1809-1847

Andante espressivo ♪= 88

17.

42

Rondo in A major

Very clear, rhythmical playing is needed for this.   The mood is cheerful throughout.
Attention to every detail of touch change and expression, with constant sense of forward
movement to the longer and stronger sounds, will gain the right interpretation.

BEETHOVEN

Allegro

from Sonatina in A

This needs sweet singing tone in the legato passages and light, crisp touch for the staccato. An important feature is the counter-melody formed by the upper notes of the accompaniment, as in bars 1, 2 and similar places. The small notes are played rapidly, beginning on the beat, throwing an accent upon the upper note which must sing along with the L.H. first quaver.

MOZART
1756-1791

Moment Musical in F minor

The mood of this piece is cheerful, playful.   Most important points are the tone
variants, which give an air of mischievous elusiveness, and strict briskness of rhythm.
Even in the *perdendosi* bit at the end let the tone *lose itself*, but not the time.

SCHUBERT, Op.94. No.3.
1797-1828

B.& Co.Ltd.19613

Arabesque in C

Here, the chief interpretative points are rising and falling tone within each arpeggio figure, and the building up to a fine climax in bars 15-18. The pedal is used to include rests, the rests being intended to enable the player to negotiate wide skips rather than to indicate *silence*.

HELLER, Op.49. No.1.
1815-1888

Mazurka

See that the semiquaver following a rest enters at its exact time spot, and trips easily
to the following note.   Notice the characteristic mazurka rhythmic accent on the second
beat, but throughout keep the normal accent on the first beat in L.H., whatever is hap-
pening elsewhere. The time-line should be flexible.

CHOPIN, Op.7. No.1.
1810-1849

B.& Co.Ltd.19613

B.& Co.Ltd.19613

Printed by Printwise (Haverhill) Limited, Suffolk 08/07 (63095)

HOURS WITH THE MASTERS
By DOROTHY BRADLEY

CONTENTS

BOSWORTH & CO. LTD.